CHRISTOPHE'S STORY

Christophe's Story copyright © Frances Lincoln Limited 2006
Text copyright © Nicki Cornwell 2006
Illustrations copyright © Karin Littlewood 2006

First published in Great Britain in 2006 and the USA in 2007
by Frances Lincoln Children's Books, 4 Torriano Mews,
Torriano Avenue, London NW5 2RZ

www.franceslincoln.com

Distributed in the USA by Publishers Group West.

British Library Cataloguing in Publication Data available on request

ISBN 10: 1-84507-521-8
ISBN 13: 978-1-84507-521-7

Printed and bound in Great Britain by Bookmarque Ltd

1 3 5 7 9 8 6 4 2

Nicki Cornwell

CHRISTOPHE'S STORY

Illustrated by
Karin Littlewood

F
FRANCES LINCOLN
CHILDREN'S BOOKS

Contents

The First Day of School

"You'll be fine!" Papa said.

Christophe looked through the gates at his new school. His legs didn't want to move.

"You remember which way you have to go?"

"Yes, Papa!"

"Smile! You look as if you have eaten bad meat!"

Christophe tried to smile.

"Good! Now off you go! Miss Finch is waiting for you!"

Forcing himself to turn away from Papa, Christophe walked across the deserted playground. He was eight years old, and he hadn't been to school for two years.

He entered the classroom. All the children turned and stared and the teacher stopped talking. She smiled at Christophe and said, "There you are!"

Christophe nodded politely. His cheeks felt as though they were burning.

"This is Christophe!" Miss Finch told the class. "He has come from a country in Africa called Rwanda, and he is joining our class. Say *good morning, Christophe*!"

"Good morning, Christophe!" the children chanted.

"Sit there, next to Greg!"

Miss Finch pointed at an empty place.

The chair scraped over the floor as Christophe pulled it towards him. Nobody spoke. He felt as if everyone was looking at him.

Miss Finch set the children some work to do, then she came to talk to Christophe.

She had eyes as blue as the sky, long silky hair the colour of corn, and pale pink skin. When she smiled, he thought that the sun had risen.

"You speak lots of languages, don't you!" she said. "Who taught you to speak English?"

"My papa did. He can speak French and English. And Kinyarwanda."

"He's a clever man! What kind of work does he do?"

"He's a doctor, but he doesn't work now."

"Oh!" said Miss Finch. She gave a little cough. Placing an open book on the table before him, she said, "You haven't been to school for a long time, have you? Don't worry, you'll soon catch up! Let's see what you can tell me about this story!"

A story? In a book? But stories shouldn't be written down! That's what Babi said!

Christophe felt sick. He stared at the black squiggly patterns of the ink on the white page.

Didn't his teacher know about stories? A storm began to blow up inside him.

"I don't like reading!" he said.

"Don't you?" Miss Finch said softly. "I'll read it to you. Watch my finger. I'll point at each of the words as I say it!"

The teacher's pink fingertip slid over the page. The words dropped from her red lips and fell like grains of sand to the ground. He listened, he watched and he waited, but nothing happened. It wasn't like the stories that Babi told! When Babi told stories Christophe saw pictures in the sky, but here in the classroom there were no pictures, only a heap of words that dropped from the teacher's mouth and piled up on the floor. Babi was right, stories shouldn't be written down!

"It will be great when you can read it for yourself!" said Miss Finch.

Why would it be great? Christophe couldn't understand what she meant!

)·O·O·O·O·(

"Greg, will you show Christophe where to go for dinner?" said Miss Finch.

Greg led Christophe to a room with tables and benches. There was a smell of food cooking that made his stomach turn over with hunger. He sat down next to Greg. Greg moved away as if he didn't want to be too close to him.

On his other side was a girl with dark curls. She gave him a sly look, whispered something to her friend, and both girls giggled. This made him feel hot and uncomfortable. He sat in silence, listening to the chatter around him. He could understand most of what was being said, but when they all talked at once, his head grew full of noise and his eyes ached.

When Christophe had finished eating, he went out into the playground with the other children. It was a cold, grey day. There was no sun, no colour in the air. Some of the boys were playing football. He didn't dare join in. What if they told him to go away?

Christophe wandered up and down by the railings. All around him, there were children laughing, jumping, and shrieking with excitement. They all had someone to play with except him. If only he were back on the side of the mountain looking after Babi's two goats! He had never felt lonely with Namo and Nmunga.

❉⦂0⦂0⦂0⦂0⦂❉

At last it was the end of the school day. Mama and Papa were there at the gates. Christophe ran to Mama and gave her a hug.

"*Comment ca va?*" said Mama.

"Speak English, Mbika," Papa said to her. "We're in England now! Is everything going well, Christophe? Is your teacher nice?"

"Yes, Papa! But she read a story from a book! Babi says you mustn't write stories down!"

"Ah, Babi!" said Papa. His eyes looked wet.

"Papa, when – when will Babi come to see me?" asked Christophe.

"Babi can't come at present, *mon petit!*"

"Why not?"

"His leg is not strong and it's a long way to come. And also there's the war!"

"I hate the war!" cried Christophe.

"*Que'est-ce qu'il dit?*" said Mama. "What did he say?"

"He says that he hates the war!" Papa said.

"Ah!" Mama's face grew heavy.

Mama and Papa were often sad. It was because of the war, or maybe it was because little Matthieu had been killed. Christophe took Mama's hand and pressed his cheek against it.

"Can we go to the park on the way home?"

Mama's face softened.

"Yes, why not!" said Papa.

Christophe saw the smile come back to her eyes and he knew that the sadness had gone. But it was sure to come back. If only he could make it go away for good!

Each day, Miss Finch made him sit down with a book. Christophe hated it! He could hear Babi's words in his ears. Babi had said to him, "Each time you tell a story, the spirit of the person who told you the story is standing behind you; and behind him there's  the spirit of the person who told him the story. And each time you tell a story, they help you to make pictures in the sky. Don't write it down, don't put it in a book, or the pictures will fade!"

Why did Miss Finch want him to do something that was wrong? A bad spirit must have got into her, that's what Babi would say!

"That's a baby book!" said a scornful voice. "It's got pictures in!" The words came from a boy with a big voice called Jeremy who was always getting told off by Miss Finch.

Christophe didn't know what to say. He felt his cheeks grow hot.

Greg looked up from his book and said, "Shove it, Jelly Knees!"

Jeremy made a rude sign with his hand and walked away.

"He's no good!" said Greg. "He supports Arsenal. What team do you support? Arsenal or Spurs?"

"Spurs!" said Christophe quickly. He had no idea what Greg meant.

"Yeah! Up with Spurs!" grinned Greg.

"Have you finished the chapter, Greg?" said Miss Finch. "No? Then you shouldn't be talking to Christophe!"

Christophe tried to focus on his book, but all he could think of was whether Greg would let him play football when they went out to the playground, and because he wasn't concentrating he was slow to finish what he had to do. That meant that he was one of the last children to join the queue for lunch, and was separated from Greg. With a sinking heart, he saw that Jeremy had followed him into the queue. Behind Jeremy were the three mean-looking boys who were always with him. They had cold, unfriendly eyes, and they reminded Christophe of especially unpleasant rats.

They sat down on the benches. Plates of spaghetti were passed down the table.

"Worms!" cried Jeremy. "That's what you eat where you come from, isn't it?"

"Yeah! That's what they eat in Africa!" tittered one of the rats.

Christophe tried to ignore them. He picked up his fork and took a mouthful of his dinner. He had just loaded up his second mouthful when Jeremy pulled a tissue out of his pocket and dropped a dead worm on to Christophe's plate.

"Have another one, seeing you like 'em so much!"

Christophe dropped his fork. He felt his stomach heave.

The rats fell about laughing.
Jeremy scooped up the worm in
his grubby fingers and shoved it
back into his pocket.

"What's the matter?"
said the dinner-lady.

"Nothing, miss!"
chorused the rats.

The rats shot little
looks at Christophe
and grinned at
each other. Then
they turned away and
ignored him. He sat all alone, his spaghetti
growing cold on the plate in front of him. He
couldn't eat another mouthful.

"You've hardly touched your dinner!" said
the dinner-lady when she came back.

"I – I don't want it!" Christophe said.

"You can leave it today, I suppose," she
grumbled, "but don't make a habit of it!
Out you go, all of you."

Greg was already out in the playground,

playing football. Christophe wrapped his arms round his chest. He was starving hungry, his stomach was rumbling. If only Greg would let him play!

The football came flying over the playground. It cannoned into his chest, almost knocking him to the ground.

Greg came running towards him.

"Sorry, Chris!" he said. "I didn't mean to hit you! Do you want to play?"

Christophe's heart did a somersault.

"Yes, please!" he said.

"Well?" said Papa.

"Was it good?" said Mama.

"I played football!" Christophe told them.

He didn't tell them about Jeremy.

The Scar

The next day Papa was in a hurry when he walked to school with Christophe. When they reached the school, the gates were still locked. There were one or two children already waiting.

"Will you be all right?" Papa said.

"Yes, Papa!" Christophe told him.

But no sooner had Papa turned the corner than Jeremy arrived, flanked by his three rats.

They began to call him names. They used words that he hadn't heard before. Christophe knew they were not good words, he knew that they meant to hurt him. He backed against the gates. He was cornered. He saw fingers poking the air, fists balling. A fire broke out in his head. He fisted his hand and lashed out at the ugly taunting lips.

Jeremy put his hand up to his mouth and backed away. Blood streamed from his lip. The rats fell back, watching their leader.

"Jelly Knees, Jelly Lips!" shouted one of the watching children.

The others took up the chant. "Jelly Knees, Jelly Lips!"

"Watch out! Bog Roll's coming!" someone called.

Christophe heard the key turn in the lock. The gates opened.

"What's going on here?" said Mr Boggis, the caretaker.

"He hit me!" cried Jeremy, pointing at Christophe. "He punched me in the mouth!

I'm going to tell Miss Finch!"

"Help yourself!" said Mr Boggis in his usual grumpy way. He opened the gates.

Jeremy flounced off.

The children began to stream through the gates. As they passed by, they smiled at Christophe as if he had done something really clever. Christophe began to feel pleased with himself.

Then Miss Finch appeared. A smug-looking Jeremy stood by her side. His lip was swollen. There were traces of dried blood round his mouth.

"Christophe, I want to speak to you!" she said. "Did you do this?" She pointed at Jeremy's face.

Christophe nodded. "Why?"

"He said things! Bad things!"

22

Christophe began to shiver. He couldn't stop.

"What did you say to Christophe, Jeremy?"

"Nothing!" said Jeremy.

"You did!" Christophe cried. "And so did the others!"

The shivering wouldn't stop.

"What others?" said Miss Finch.

Christophe pointed at the three rats.

"Four against one? That's bullying!" said Miss Finch.

She kept Jeremy and the rats in at break, but she sent Christophe out to play.

"You're very quiet, Christophe!" said Papa that night. "Is anything wrong?"

Christophe didn't want to tell Papa, but somehow it all fell out of him. He cried, he couldn't stop himself. Papa held him tight and he told Papa everything that had happened.

When there were no more tears to come,

they sat quietly together. The room had grown dark. The pale face of the moon looked in through the open window.

"Papa, why did they pick on me?" he said.

Papa shrugged his shoulders. His eyes glistened. They were full of tears. Christophe tugged at Papa's arm.

"You didn't answer me, Papa! Why does that boy hate me? Why does he want to hurt me?"

"*C'est pareil partout!*" Papa said sadly. "It's the same everywhere! Here, it's because of the colour of your skin. In our country, it's because you are Hutu or Tutsi. In other places, it's because of what you believe."

"But why, Papa? Why?"

"It's because people do not know how to be of equal worth! There is always someone who wants to be on top! They say 'I'm better than you. I'm worth more than you. I should have everything and you should have nothing'."

"But that's not fair!" said Christophe.

"I know it's not fair. But that doesn't stop them!"

"I hit him!" Christophe said. "I made his lip bleed. Was that wrong?"

"That's a difficult question. When you meet someone like that, you've got two choices. You fight, or you run away. If I hadn't run away, I'd be dead!"

"I hit him!"

"Did that make you feel better?"

"Yes!"

"Ah well! We must each deal with these things in our own way, I suppose!" Papa sighed. "Sleep now, *mon petit*!"

He drew the curtain over the face of the listening moon.

Christophe went to school the next day with a scared feeling in his stomach, wondering if Jeremy would pick on him. Every so often their eyes met, and Jeremy gave Christophe a dirty look, but he made no attempt to threaten Christophe, nor did the three rats. After a few days, Christophe began to hope that Jeremy would leave him alone now, but he never felt quite sure.

Little by little, he began to get used to the new school. He made friends, first with the footballers, then with some of the other children in the class. But Greg, freckle-faced Greg with his wide smile, was Christophe's special friend.

At first he struggled with the work that Miss Finch gave him. Christophe hadn't been to school for two years, and he had forgotten everything he had done in his first school. There all the lessons were in French, and now they were in English. He could only just understand what he had to do. Mama and Papa said to try his best, and it would all come right, but sometimes

Christophe wondered if they might be wrong.

Then, one day, something clicked. Christophe worked out how to put together the string of letters that made a word. It wasn't long before he was reading all sorts of things – labels and notices, worksheets and instructions, or books of facts that Miss Finch called 'reference books'. But he wouldn't read stories. He was so sure that stories shouldn't be in books that he wouldn't even try to read them.

"Is that all you've read?" said Miss Finch.

Christophe hung his head.

"Is anything the matter?"

"I don't like the story!" he said.

Miss Finch told him to put it back and choose another one, but that didn't help. He stared out of the window and dreamed beautiful dreams instead.

"Christophe, you're dreaming!" said Miss Finch.

"Sorry, Miss!" he said.

He couldn't tell her what was wrong.

One lunchtime when they were playing football, he was the goalkeeper and Pete (who was one of the footballers) tried for a goal. Christophe saw the ball flying towards him. He jumped sideways. He felt the ball ricochet off his fingers, then he landed stomach-first on the playground floor. For a moment, he couldn't breathe. It was as if all the breath had been knocked out of him.

"Are you all right, Chris?" asked Pete.

"Uh!" Christophe's breath began to come back. He breathed in and out, in and out. Strange, harsh, wheezing noises came from his chest. He slipped his hand under his vest and his shirt and ran it over his ribs. "Ouch!"

"Let's have a look!" said Greg.

He reached for Christophe's shirt so that he could see for himself.

"Get off!" cried Christophe, and he pushed Greg away.

"I'm only trying to see what's the matter!" cried Greg.

Christophe felt his vest and his shirt being torn out of his hands. He felt the cool breeze on his skin. He saw their faces screw up, their eyes darken. They were both staring at something on his skin.

Just above his waist was a long, raised lump. It looked as if someone had stuck a piece of purple-brown playdoh on Christophe's body, but it wasn't stuck on, it was part of him. He knew what it looked like. He had seen it often enough in the mirror.

"What's that?" Pete said uncertainly.

"It's a scar!" Christophe said sullenly.

The other footballers crowded round. They all talked at once.

"Does it hurt?"

"What does it feel like?"

"Can I touch it?" said Greg.

Christophe nodded.

Greg prodded the lump.

"It's hard!" he said. "How did you get it?"

"I got it from a bullet," Christophe told them. He felt angry. He didn't like them staring. He pulled down his vest.

"Come off it! Bullets make holes!" said Pete.

"It was a bullet! Ask my papa if you don't believe me! The bullet didn't go in me. It went past so fast that it burned me!" His eyes were smarting. He was afraid he was going to cry!

"Who shot you?" asked Greg.

"A soldier!" said Christophe.

"Why?"

"Because of the war!"

"What war?" asked Greg.

The bell rang.

"Line up, please!" said the dinner-lady.

* * *

"You had a lot to talk about!" said Miss Finch.

"Christophe was telling us about his scar! Show Miss Finch your scar, Christophe!" said Greg.

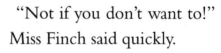

"Not if you don't want to!" Miss Finch said quickly.

"It's all right!" he said.

Christophe lifted his shirt and vest. He saw shock on Miss Finch's face. She smiled, but it wasn't a very good smile. It looked as if she had borrowed someone else's.

"He was shot by a bullet!" said Greg.

"He was fighting in the war!" said Pete.

"No, I wasn't!" said Christophe indignantly.

"What war?" said one of the girls.

"Slow down," said Miss Finch. "If you want to talk about war that's fine by me, but you must stop pestering Christophe with questions. What happens when there's a war? Think hard, everyone!"

"People fight," said someone. "And sometimes they get killed!"

"Yes! Now why do you think they fight?"

"Because one side picks on the other!"

"Why would they do that?" asked Miss Finch.

"I know!" cried Pete. "Because the other side has got something they want!"

"Good!" said Miss Finch. "Any more ideas? Christophe, you've got your hand up."

"My papa says it's because there is always someone who wants to be on top! They pick on someone and they say 'I'm better than you. I'm worth more than you. I should have everything and you should have nothing!' And they kill people who don't do what they say. My papa says either you fight or you run away and sometimes it's good to run away!"

"Your papa's a clever man!" said Miss Finch softly.

****

That night he went running to meet Papa.

"Papa, they saw my scar!" he said.

"Oh?" said Papa.

"I didn't want to show them, but they made me!"

"Did they?" frowned Papa.

"It was all right, Papa. I didn't mind! They asked me what happened and I told them I was shot, and they didn't believe me! So I said, 'Talk to my papa! My papa will tell you!' Then they believed me! How's Mama?"

"She's resting!"

"Is she all right?" asked Christophe.

"Yes, she's fine. She's tired, that's all! That baby in her tummy is growing quite big now. It's hard work making a baby!"

"I know! I watched Nmunga making a baby. She got ever so fat! Like this!"

He stretched out his hands to show Papa how big Nmunga had grown.

"Is Babi coming yet?"

"No!"

Papa's eyes went dark.

"Come on, Papa!" Christophe said quickly. "Race you to the end of the road!"

Miss Finch Gets it Wrong

The next day it was raining. At playtime they had to go into the hall. Children came running up to Christophe. They wanted to see his scar. They wanted to know who had shot him. They clustered round him like dogs waiting to be fed. He felt a bit scared, and he was relieved when Miss Finch appeared. She was carrying a notepad and a pen.

"Christophe's going to tell us how he got shot, Miss Finch! Tell us, Christophe!"

"Slow down!" she said. "Do you want to tell them, Christophe?"

Christophe looked at their hungry faces. They didn't want to listen to Miss Finch. They wanted to listen to him! Even Jeremy and the rats were standing there waiting for him to speak! Christophe felt important. He didn't feel scared any more.

"Yes!" he said.

He told the children how he was in the house with his papa and his mama when the bad men came.

"They looked really scary. They were dressed in banana leaves and they had chalked their faces white. They carried knives and spears, and they burst into the house. They told my papa that they'd come to set him free!"

As the words poured out of his mouth, the school hall vanished. Christophe was back in his own home in Rwanda. He could see the bad men as clearly as if they stood there before him. He saw his mama cowering on the bed. He felt the sweatiness of her hand. He knew they were bad men. He wanted Papa to say no. But Papa didn't – Papa went off with them!

"Mama told me they were soldiers."

"Soldiers?" said Pete. "They couldn't be!"

"They were!" Christophe insisted. "Papa went with them, he had to. Then they came back. This time they were wearing their uniforms. Mama said, 'Run, Christophe, run!'

So I ran, but one of the soldiers saw me. He fired at me, and I fell!"

He fell to the floor, clutching his side.

"Did it hurt?"

"Yes!" said Christophe.

"Did you go to the doctor?"

"I couldn't. We had to hide!"

Then he told them how the night went red with flames. The soldiers had set fire to his house.

"Why?"

"Because they were angry with Papa!" said Christophe.

"Why?"

"Did he rob a bank?" asked Pete.

"No!" Christophe said angrily. "My papa's a good man! The soldiers are bad! Papa won't do what the soldiers tell him to do. He ran away from them!

So the soldiers burned
our house down!"

"Why didn't the police
stop them?"

"Police, soldiers! Soldiers,
police!" He shrugged. "Same thing!
No difference!"

The bell rang.

"Sorry!" said Miss Finch. She
stopped writing. "Christophe, you'll
have to stop there. The bell's gone!
Everyone line up now, please!"

After school, Christophe was impatient for Papa to come. He wanted to tell him all about it. When at last Papa came, he said, "Papa, I told the children how I got shot!"

"Yes?"

"And I told them about the soldiers and the war. I showed them how the soldier shot me!" He dropped on one knee and squeezed the trigger. "And then how I fell!" He dropped face down to the ground. That was the bit he liked best! "Papa, I want to be a storyteller like Babi!"

"Why not, *mon petit*? If you work hard, you can be anything!"

He saw Papa smile, but there wasn't any sun in Papa's eyes. They looked cloudy, the way the sky often looked in England.

❖

At playtime the next day Miss Finch said, "Christophe, I want you to stay behind for a moment. Don't worry, you're not in trouble!"

She put some papers in front of him. "Will you read this to me?"

They were stapled together like a book. Christophe felt a sharp pain in his chest. The bad spirit had got back into Miss Finch!

"It's too difficult!" he cried. He hadn't even looked at the words.

"Try it, please try it!" pleaded Miss Finch. He saw a funny little smile on her face. "It's a fantastic story!"

"It can't be!" he cried. "It's a story in a book! A story should be kept in the head and told from the mouth! That's what Babi says, and he knows about stories! He's a storyteller!"

He pushed the papers away and leapt out of his chair.

"This is how you tell a story, like this! You have the story in your head, and when you tell it, you use a big voice or a little voice. And you tell it with your hands, like this! And when you finish, the story flies back into your head. Like a bird going back to its nest!"

"Oh!" said Miss Finch. "But this story is

different! Try it, Christophe, please try it!"

"All right then."

Christophe gave a big sigh. He sat down by Miss Finch and looked down at the pages, but he had only read a few, slow words when he felt his heart begin to thump. His eyes filled with tears, the words on the page grew fuzzy.

"This is my story!" he cried. "You've taken my words!"

"I know it's your story!" protested Miss Finch. "I wrote down what you told the other children, and I haven't changed a word. Last night I typed it up and printed it out. This is

for you. This is your copy!"

"I don't need a copy!" cried Christophe. "I've got it in my head!"

He scrumpled up the papers and threw them at the bin.

"Christophe, I'm sorry," Miss Finch said. "I didn't mean to make you angry!"

He pushed her hand away.

"You don't understand!" he cried. "Stories are alive! You mustn't put them in books or the pictures will go! That's what Babi says! I wish he would come! *Je me souhaite qu'il pourrait te dire!*"

He burst into tears.

"Christophe, who is Babi?"

"He's – he's my mama's papa! If only he would come!"

"Where is he?"

"In Rwanda!" he sobbed. He couldn't stop himself crying.

Miss Finch handed him a tissue.

Christophe blew his nose and struggled to calm himself. Miss Finch was kind. She hadn't meant to upset him. She didn't understand about stories, that was all!

"I'm sorry! I shouldn't have written your story down without asking you!" she said.

Christophe gave a big sniff.

"You really do hate stories in books, don't you!"

"Yes. They go slow, slow, slow! It's boring!

When Babi tells a story, you want to sing and dance and play! And sometimes it's scary and you feel sick or you want to hit someone!"

"That's the way I felt when I heard your story," said Miss Finch softly.

Christophe looked into her sky-blue eyes. There was no bad spirit in her. There never had been.

"I'm sorry I threw it away!" he said.

Miss Finch went quiet. Christophe wondered if she was angry with him. She had worked so hard. She had tried to help him, and he'd torn up her work and thrown it away!

Then she said, "Babi is right, storytelling is very important. Why don't we do a project on storytelling in the class?"

"Yes, please!" smiled Christophe.

"Do you think you could help me?" she asked

"Me? How?"

"Some of the children have heard your story, others haven't. Do you think you could tell your story to the whole class?"

Christophe nodded eagerly. He could show them how he was shot. He was really good at the 'falling on the floor' bit!

"You don't have to if you don't want to!" said Miss Finch.

"I do want to!" replied Christophe.

"Are you sure?"

"Yes!"

"When would you like to do it?"

"Now," he said. "Could we do it now?"

"I don't see why not!" smiled Miss Finch. "Shall I make a tape recording? Then you'll be able to listen to yourself telling it, if you want to!"

Christophe nodded. That wasn't the same as writing it down!

When the children came back from break, Miss Finch said, "We are now going to do a project on storytelling! Is there anyone here who doesn't like stories?" No hands went up.

"What, everyone likes stories?"

"Yes!"

"I like scary ones!" said Pete.

"I don't," said Gemma. "I like stories that make me laugh! If they're really scary, I feel sick!"

"How can you be scared if they're not real? They're made up, aren't they!" said Pete.

"Some of them are," said Miss Finch, "but some of them aren't. I'm going to ask Christophe to tell you a story!"

"Christophe?"

"Is he going to tell us about the war?"

"He's going to tell you the story of how he came to this country," said Miss Finch. "Come to the front of the class, Christophe!"

Christophe went up to stand beside Miss Finch. He saw rows of eyes. Everyone was looking at him. Everyone was waiting for him to speak.

"Over to you, Christophe!" said Miss Finch.

The words had gone. He felt panic spread through him. Without the words there would be no story. What would Babi say? He had got the chance to be a storyteller and he couldn't find the words!

He heard Babi's voice, as clearly as if Babi had been there. *There's a bad spirit holding on to your tongue. Open your mouth, push out the words, and your tongue will be free!*

He swallowed, opened his mouth and forced out the words.

"This is the story of how I came to this country," he said.

Christophe's Story

"One night, my papa comes back from work with clouds in his face. My mama says, *'What's the matter?'*"

He deepened his voice to show how Papa spoke.

"*'They want me to see with their eyes and to speak with their mouths!'* says Papa. Papa's fists go tight, like he wants to hit someone.

Mama gasps. She can't find her words. She holds the baby tight.

Papa says, *'I've got eyes of my own, and I can't speak with someone else's mouth. There's going to be trouble!'*

Mama starts to shake.

Papa puts his arms round her and says, *'We've got to get out!'*"

Christophe used a lighter, softer, scared voice for Mama.

"'*Out? What do you mean, out!*' says Mama.

'*Out of the country!*' Papa tells her.

'*What, leave all my friends?*'

'*If we stay, we're going to get killed! We'll go to Babi's village! That's what we'll do!*' Papa says. '*Then we'll cross the border and go to Europe.*'

'*Europe?*' says Mama. '*That's a long way to go!*'

Then we hear the drums!"

Christophe began to beat out a rhythm on Miss Finch's table. The words were coming more easily now. The children sat there, round-eyed.

"Papa sucks his breath in. He says, '*I didn't think they'd come that quick!*'

Mama says, '*Run!*'

'*It's too late!*' Papa cries.

I say, '*Who's coming? What's happening?*'

But they're not listening to me. My heart's going up and down like it's going to jump out of my mouth. Something bad is going to happen, and I don't know what it is.

Tatatum! Tatatum!

The drums get louder.

Papa wants to run. But he can't. He's stuck to the floor. Mama cries, '*What are we going to do?*' A whistle blows! Pheeeew!"

Christophe banged on the cupboard door and pushed it open.

"The door breaks down! They burst into the room! This is what they look like!"

Christophe picked up blackboard chalk and dragged it over his brown skin. His brown eyes glared out of a scary white mask. He grabbed a ruler. Then he began to jig up and down, brandishing the ruler like a chopper.

"They have white faces, like this! And they wear banana leaves! And they carry spears and big knives!

'*Kubohoza!*' they cry. '*We've come to set you free!*'

Papa pushes Mama away from him so they won't hurt her. She falls on the bed. She's still holding little Matthieu. The tears are rolling down her cheeks, but Papa doesn't look at her. He acts like she's not there. And he doesn't look at me.

'*I'm coming!*' he says. And he goes with the men.

I'm scared. I don't like these men. I think they will hurt Papa. I start to cry.

'*Where's Papa gone?*' I say. '*Why did he go with those bad men?*'

Mama is crying, crying, crying, like she can't turn off a tap. She says, '*Papa had to go. They're soldiers, those men. Papa had to go with them, act like they're his friends. If he didn't go with them, they'd kill him!*'

Matthieu's crying. I'm crying. Mama's crying. We're all crying. Mama tells me I mustn't go to school, and I mustn't go out to play. I've got to stay in the house.

For three days we wait. Mama doesn't dare go out and we've got no food in the house. My tummy is grumbling away. My mama hasn't got enough milk for Matthieu and he won't stop crying.

Then Ayombe comes. She's Mama's friend. She brings a can of milk and some bananas and some sweetcorn, and I can't stop eating.

Matthieu drinks a bit of milk and he stops crying. Mama asks what's happened to Papa. Ayombe doesn't know. Mama starts crying all over again.

Ayombe keeps bringing us food. Mama won't let me go out. I'm mad at the men for taking Papa away and I'm scared they're going to hurt him. Each night I go to sleep and hope that Papa is coming back, but when I wake up in the morning he still isn't there.

Then we hear the drums. It's not a *kubohoza* sound, it's the other drums, the ones that tell you what's going on. Mama listens to them and she says, '*Papa's got away. Quick! The soldiers are coming back!*'

She throws Matthieu over her shoulder and ties the cloth round him.

We look out of the window. No one's there yet. We open the door. The sun is going down. There are shadows everywhere. We can hear noises and shouting.

'*Run!*' says Mama. We run between the houses. There's more shouting. It's the soldiers! Then one of the soldiers sees me. He drops on his knee, like this! He fires his gun! And the bullet hits me!"

Christophe fell to the floor, clutching his side. He heard the children gasp. That was definitely the best bit!

"I – I don't know what's going on! It's like I've fallen asleep!

I wake up in Ayombe's bed. '*What's happened?*' I say. My voice is all tired and squeaky.

Ayombe says, '*You're a lucky boy, Christophe! A bullet came looking for you, but it didn't find you. It rushed by so fast that it burned you. Just there, on the side of your body!*'

I say, *'Lucky? I'm not lucky! I'm hurting all over!'*

She says, *'You're lucky you didn't die!'*

And this is what it did to me!"

Christophe lifted up his shirt and his vest and showed off his bullet burn.

"Wow!" gasped the children.

Christophe felt a grin beginning to spread over his face. No, he mustn't smile! It was no time to smile now!

"Next the sky outside goes red. Ayombe goes running to the window. There are flames shooting up to the sky.

'They've set fire to your house!' she cries.

I want to see the fire, but my legs won't work.

Mama says, '*You stay right there!*'

Then I see that my brother isn't there. '*Where's Matthieu?*' I ask."

For a moment, Christophe couldn't find his words. Don't think of Matthieu, think of Babi, he told himself! He made his voice firm.

"My mama starts to cry. Rain is falling from her eyes. Ayombe puts her arms round Mama. She's crying, too.

'*He wasn't so lucky,*' said Ayombe. '*A bullet got him!*'

The fire dies down. The shouting stops. No one comes chasing after us.

'*What you going to do?*' says Ayombe.

'*We'll go to Babi, that's what we'll do,*' Mama says. '*We'll get a place on the bus tomorrow.*'

'*How will you pay?*' says Ayombe.

'*I've got money!*' says Mama. She pats the side of her body, here! She's got a purse that Papa gave her. It's under her clothes where no one can see it.

'*Mama!*' I say. I'm thinking of Papa. How is he going to find us?

Mama knows what I'm thinking. She says, '*Don't worry, Christophe! Papa will come and find us as soon as he can!*'

But I can see clouds in Mama's face, and I know she's scared.

The next day we say goodbye to Ayombe and we go on the bus. It's a long, long way. We have to keep changing buses. I keep falling asleep and waking up again. I'm hot and I'm hurting all over. I'm having bad dreams. I dream that Papa's looking for me and he can't find me.

Then we get to Babi's village. Babi comes. Mama starts crying."

Christophe began to weep and wring his hands just as his mother had done.

'*They shot my children!*' she says. '*Matthieu's dead, and Christophe's sick. He needs a doctor! Oh, why isn't his papa here!*'

'*Don't cry! I'll fix him!*' Babi tells her.

He picks me up and carries me to his house. Mama's crying again.

He puts leaves and things where it hurts — here and here! Then he gives me a hot drink. It tastes horrible! Papa never gave me medicine like that! I fall asleep, and when I wake up my head isn't hot any more.

When I'm better, Babi says, '*You want to come out with Namo and Nmunga?*'

So Babi and I walk on the mountain with Namo and Nmunga, and we help them to find something to eat. It's hot. All day long the sun

burns the earth. We walk when the goats walk, and we rest when they rest. And Babi tells me stories. He's my mama's papa. He knows lots and lots of stories. He's a storyteller. He's got hair like mine, but it's white, and he walks with a stick because one leg is always tired. When his leg is very tired, he lets me take Namo and Nmunga out all by myself. He knows I'll bring them back safely!

I don't go to school any more because there isn't one. I go out with Namo and Nmunga instead.

Then Papa's friends come. They say Papa is waiting for us across the border. Babi won't come with us. He says he'll wait till his leg gets better.

So we say goodbye to Babi, then we walk over the mountains. Papa's friends show us where to go. It's cold at night. We make a fire and we wrap ourselves in blankets and sleep by it. And then we find Papa. He's very thin and he's got a bad leg just like Babi.

Mama says, '*What happened to your leg?*'

Papa says, '*Never mind my leg, I'm lucky to be alive!*' Then he says, '*Mbika, you've got to learn to speak English now! We're going to England!*'

We go on buses and on trains, and we stay in lots of different houses. Some smell horrible! And every day Papa is teaching me English.

Then we get on an aeroplane and we come to England. And now I can go to school again! It was horrible at first because I didn't know anybody and I didn't have any friends. But it's better now.

Papa says that when the fighting stops, we'll go back home. Maybe I'll see some of my old friends, maybe I won't.

And that's the story of how I came to this country!"

Christophe looked at the faces in front of him. They were all – what was that word? Gob-smacked! Even Jeremy and the rats looked at him as if he was someone big and important.

"Phew!" said Greg.

Miss Finch began to clap. The children joined in. They drummed their feet on the floor and their fists on the desks. Then Miss Finch said, "Was that a scary story?"

"Yes!" chorused the children.

"And it was real!" said Miss Finch. "But Christophe is not the only one who has a story to tell. You've all got stories inside you! Maybe it's a story about a pet, or your brother or sister, or something that happened to you. Maybe it's funny, maybe it's scary! Get into pairs, and as soon as you find a story in your head, you can share it with the person who is sitting next to you. Take turns to tell your story and to listen to your friends! And don't forget to talk with your hands and your face, as well as your mouth!"

Christophe watched as the children formed pairs. He felt very tired. He looked over their heads and saw a brown, wrinkled face smiling at him from the back of the classroom. He heard Babi's voice say, *It's your turn to tell the stories, now! I've got to go! Goodbye, Christophe!*

The face vanished. He blinked. He rubbed his eyes. Babi wasn't there. He had imagined it!

▶◀◎▶◀◎▶◀◎▶◀◎

At the end of school, Papa was waiting for him by the gates.

"Papa!" he cried. "I told my story to everyone in the class!"

"Well done, *mon petit*, well done!"

They began to walk away from the school.

"And, Papa, I thought I saw Babi! I thought

I saw him at the back of the class. He said it was my turn to tell the stories now!"

"Did he?" said Papa quietly.

"But he wasn't really there!"

Papa wasn't listening! Papa's eyes were cloudy. Something had happened, something bad!

"What's the matter? What's happened, Papa?"

Papa stopped walking. He took hold of Christophe by the shoulders. Papa's hands were shaking. Something was very wrong.

"Babi has died, Christophe!"

"No, Papa, no!" he wailed.

"Babi was too tired to go on living, Christophe!"

"I should have stayed with him! His leg didn't hurt when I took the goats out for him! If I'd stayed with him, he would be all right!"

Papa slowly shook his head. "You can't walk between someone and their death, *mon petit!*" he said. "Babi is gone. You'll have to be the storyteller now, Christophe!"

Christophe felt like a choked-up river. "Papa, I want to cry and I can't!" he wailed.

"Your tears will come!" Papa said sadly.

The Story is Told Again

A few days later, Miss Finch said to Christophe, "Would you like more people to hear your story?"

He nodded eagerly.

"How would you feel about telling it to the whole school?"

He imagined standing at the end of the hall with all the big children looking at him. That wasn't the same as standing in front of the class. A horrible, sick feeling got into his stomach. There was no way he could do it.

"I couldn't!" he said.

"I'm not surprised!" said Miss Finch. "But you'd like them to hear it, wouldn't you?"

"Yes!"

"There is a way we could make that happen. I could read it to them. But to do that, I'd have to write down the tape recording that

I made when you told the class. And I know what you think about that!"

Write it down? Christophe flinched. Babi would say no! Don't do it!

"I can't use the tape recording itself, there are too many background noises! The only way is to write it down," said Miss Finch. "It's up to you, Christophe. If you don't want me to do it, I won't!"

Christophe stood there, trying to think it through. If he said no, none of the big children would get to hear the story. Or the rest of the teachers. And he wanted to tell them. He wanted them to know what had happened! But what would Babi say? And what would happen to the pictures?

"Talk to your parents," said Miss Finch. "No need to decide now!"

"Papa!" Christophe said. "Miss Finch wants to write down my story so she can read it to the big children!"

"Does she?"

"But Babi said stories shouldn't be written down!"

"Yes?"

"Papa, what shall I tell Miss Finch?"

"You want me to tell you what's right?"

"Yes, Papa!"

"Christophe, *mon petit*, I can't tell you what to do. You're the storyteller now! You've got to speak with your own mouth. If your heart tells you no, don't do it! But if your heart tells you yes, then that's what you should do!"

Christophe went to bed. He couldn't get to sleep. What was he going to say to Miss Finch?

If only Babi would tell him what to do! But he would never see Babi again.

He felt a terrible pain in his heart. It was quite different from the pain that he had felt when he had been shot. He felt as if he were bursting apart. Babi had gone, and so had Matthieu.

Then the tears came. They streamed out of his eyes and poured down his face. He buried his face in his pillow and pulled his duvet over his head. He didn't want anyone to hear him crying.

Little by little the pain went away. His tears dried up, and his head grew cool. He knew what had to be done. He must tell Miss Finch to write his story down. Babi would say that the more people who heard it, the better. Maybe the pictures would still be there.

Then Christophe fell asleep.

A couple of weeks later, all the children were in

assembly. Mama and Papa came to the school and sat by Mrs Crowther, the Head Teacher. Mama spread over the edges of her chair. She was getting very big now. Christophe didn't sit by them. He had chosen to sit by Greg and Pete.

Miss Finch said, "I'm going to tell you a story about a boy who used to live in a place called Rwanda, in Africa. He is now an asylum-seeker in England, and he goes to this school. This is his story, in his own words."

Then she read Christophe's story. Everyone sat very still. Sometimes small gasps were heard when the story got scary. When Miss Finch had finished, Christophe thought the clapping would never come to an end. He felt shy and strange, but at the same time he felt good. And he knew that the pictures hadn't gone away. They were still there, shining into the hearts and minds of the children.

Papa stood up and said, "I am very happy! My son is very clever! Thank you for helping him!"

Mama didn't say anything. He saw that her eyes were very bright. From time to time she wiped them with her handkerchief.

"Was that OK?" Miss Finch asked Christophe when it was all over.

"Yes!" he said. "But it's better when I tell it myself!"

"That's right!" said Miss Finch. "But how

many children can you tell? And what about the ones who don't go to your school? Why don't we see if we can make your story into a book, with lots and lots of copies, so that anyone can read it? Even if they live in another country!"

And that's exactly what happened!

By the time the book was published, Christophe's little sister had been born. Christophe sat holding her hand while Mama gave her milk.

Mama's face shone. All the sadness had gone. She said, "Now you've got someone else to listen to your story!"

Footnote

Khubohoza means "to help set you free." It sounds good, but it isn't. The men who used it were bullies who wanted others to do as they say. They rubbed white chalk on their faces, and dressed in banana leaves to make themselves look scary. Then they burst into your house waving spears and big knives. They pretended that someone else was bullying you, and they acted as if they had come to set you free. You knew that if you didn't go with them, you would be in trouble.

More books from Frances Lincoln

Butter-Finger

Bob Cattell and John Agard
Illustrated by Pam Smy

Riccardo Small may not be a great cricketer –
he's only played twice before for Calypso Cricket Club –
but he's mad about the game and can tell you
the averages of every West Indies cricketer in history.
His other love is writing calypsos. Today is Riccardo's
chance to make his mark with Calypso CC
against The Saints. The game goes right down to the wire
with captain, Natty and team-mates, Bashy and Leo
striving for victory, but then comes the moment
that changes everything for Riccardo…

ISBN 10: 1-84507-376-2
ISBN 13: 978-1-84507-376-3

The Great Tug of War

Beverley Naidoo
Illustrated by Piet Grobler

Mmutla the hare is a mischievous trickster.
When Tswhene the baboon is vowing to throw you
off a cliff, you need all the tricks you can think of!
When Mmutla tricks Tlou the elephant
and Kubu the hippo into having an epic tug-of-war,
the whole savanna is soon laughing at their foolishness.
However, small animals should not make fun
of big animals and King Lion sets out to teach
cheeky little Mmutla a lesson…

These tales are the African origins of
America's beloved stories of Brer Rabbit.
Their warm humour is guaranteed to enchant
new readers of all ages.

ISBN 10: 1-84507-055-0
ISBN 13: 978-1-84507-055-7

Purple Class and the Skelington

Sean Taylor
Illustrated by Helen Bate
Cover illustrated by Polly Dunbar

Meet Purple Class – there is Jamal who often
forgets his reading book, Ivette who is the best in the class
at everything, Yasmin who is sick on every school trip,
Jodie who owns a crazy snake called Slinkypants,
Leon who is great at rope-swinging,
Shea who knows all about blood-sucking slugs
and Zina who makes a rather disturbing discovery
in the teacher's chair…

Has Mr Wellington died? Purple Class is sure
he must have done when they find a skeleton
sitting in his chair. Is this Mr Wellington's skelington?
What will they say to the school inspector?
Featuring a calamitous cast of classmates,
the adventures of Purple Class will make you
laugh out loud in delight.

ISBN 10: 1-84507-377-0
ISBN 13: 978-1-84507-377-0

Roar, Bull, Roar!

Andrew Fusek Peters and Polly Peters
Illustrated by Anke Weckmann

What is the real story of the ghostly Roaring Bull?
Who is the batty old lady in the tattered clothes?
Why is the new landlord such a nasty piece of work?

Czech brother and sister Jan and Marie arrive in
rural England in the middle of the night – and not
everyone is welcoming. As they try to settle into their
new school, they are plunged into a series of mysteries.
Old legends are revived as Jan and Marie unearth
shady secrets in a desperate bid to save their family
from eviction. In their quest, they find unlikely allies
and deadly enemies – who will stop at nothing
to keep the past buried.

ISBN 10: 1-84507-520-X
ISBN 13: 978-1-84507-520-0

Dear Whiskers

Ann Whitehead Nagda
Illustrated by Stephanie Roth

Everyone in Jenny's class has to write
a letter to someone in another class.
Only you have to pretend to be a mouse!
Jenny thinks the whole thing is really silly...
until her penfriend writes back. There is
something mysterious about Jenny's penfriend.
Will Jenny discover her secret?

ISBN 10: 1-84507-563-3
ISBN 13: 978-1-84507-563-7